THE COQUÍES STILL SING

This book is dedicated to my parents, Luis and Maritza, who personify compassion and tenacity every single day.

Special thanks to: Charlotte Sheedy, for your unwavering support, guidance, and kindness, and your commitment to social justice and culturally responsive children's literature. My deepest gratitude to the talented network of women who have been a part of this book's journey: Connie Hsu, Luisa Beguiristaín, Krystal Quiles, Amparo Ortiz, Mercedes Padró, and Jen Keenan. Thank you, Rachel Abrams and Jordyn Smith, for your guidance and clarity during my story-writing process and beyond. To Aaron—the daily joy you infuse into my life is embedded in these pages. Lastly, thank *you*, dear reader, for welcoming this story into your world. —K. N. G.

Dedicated to the memories of my Grandma Cielo and Mamita Ana. —K. Q.

Published by Roaring Brook Press
Roaring Brook Press is a division of Holtzbrinck Publishing Holdings Limited Partnership
120 Broadway, New York, NY 10271 • mackids.com

Back matter photos courtesy of Karina Nicole González and Krystal Quiles.

Our books may be purchased in bulk for promotional, educational, or business use. Please contact your local bookseller or the Macmillan Corporate and Premium Sales Department at (800) 221-7945 ext. 5442 or by email at MacmillanSpecialMarkets@macmillan.com.

Library of Congress Cataloging-in-Publication Data is available.

First edition, 2022
Book design by Mercedes Padró
The illustrations in this book were created using gouache and acrylics on a variety of papers and finished digitally. The text was set in NeutraText.
Printed in China by RR Donnelley Asia Printing Solutions Ltd., Dongguan City, Guangdong Province

ISBN 978-1-250-78718-7
1 3 5 7 9 10 8 6 4 2

THE COQUÍES STILL SING

story by
Karina Nicole González

illustrations by
Krystal Quiles

ROARING BROOK PRESS
New York

At sunup, I climb the ladder to the roof.
From here, I am as tall as Abuela's mango tree.
Its branches, heavy with fruit, reach out to say hello.
"Hola," I reply, giving the branch a shake.
Ripened mangoes rain down onto the garden with gentle thuds.

The mango tree gives us many gifts.
When the sun is high, its leaves lend
their cool shade.
When I'm hungry, its fruit is the
sweetest snack.

And when night falls, a song fills the air.
CO-QUÍ, CO-QUÍ, CO-QUÍ
Hidden in the garden live the coquí frogs.
Luna runs in circles, barking and dancing to their tune.
"Co-quí, co-quí. Oh, how I love thee,"
    I sing back.
        "You sound just like your mother,"
        Abuela says.
            Suddenly, a strong wind blows, lifting
            the coquíes' song away.

Every evening, Papi sits at the kitchen table
listening to the radio.
   But tonight, music isn't playing. A reporter is
talking about a storm.
   "Hurricane," she says.
   The words come in pieces, fighting through static.
"... *making landfall* ..."
"... *stay safe* ..."

HURACÁN

My little brother, Benito, cries,
and my heart races.
But Papi has a plan.

Benito and Abuela search for
flashlights and candles.
I shut the windows.
Papi seals the doors.

The rain falls, drumming a steady beat on the metal roof.
Luna bounces at my feet.
"Don't worry, Lunita. I will protect you," I say, pulling her close.
The howling wind slams against the windows.

I grip Papi's hands, and he whispers in my ear,
"Co-quí, co-quí. Oh, how I love thee."

I peek through a slit in the shutter.
CRACK! A branch snaps, falling against our house.
"The mango tree!" I scream.
Papi pulls me away and guides me to the closet.

Inside, Abuela and Benito are sheltering.
We huddle together as the house shakes.
Luna shivers in my arms.
Abuela prays through the howling wind, her
heart beating against my chest.

With one giant gust, the roof lifts up and away.
Rain gushes in.

Hours pass, and the rain stops,
turning everything quiet.
We are wet and scared,
but we are alive.

There's no electricity or running water.
Trees have fallen everywhere,
blocking the safe road.

Our garden is gone, too.
The mango tree stands
brown and bare.

Little by little, we remove the fallen trees.
My strong arms help me carry buckets of freshwater.
But time passes slowly.
At sundown, the coquíes' song is silent.
I sing to them instead, hoping they
will hear me.

"Co-quí, co-quí.
Oh, how I love thee."

Papi tells me, "They will come
back and so will all of this."

"We will always have each other," says Abuela.
"Seeds, too," says our neighbor Don Rafael.
He hands me a fistful of vegetable seeds and says,
"This is our gold."

The garden becomes our gathering place.
A place where seeds of hope are planted.
A place where food is shared with our neighbors.
A place where laughter can be heard once again.

But some nights, I cry.
I think about my friends who have moved away.
We never said goodbye.
I think about Papi and Abuela.
With each passing day, their energy fades.

I notice how the mango tree stands brown and bare.
Yet it stands.
My school's doors are closed forever.
Yet my teachers taught me that books can open any door.

At night, our neighborhood is without light.
Yet we can see the moon and the stars more clearly than ever.
I hold on to what I have—
my smile,
my community,
and my family—
because my roots
are strong.

Months later, glimpses of green return.

"Elenita!" Abuela calls.

Buds sprout from an old branch of the mango tree.

Soon, its leaves will lend their cool shade, and sweet fruit will hang from its branches.

"The tree is strong like you, Elena," Abuela says.

"Like our pueblo," I say. "Nothing can knock us down."

I open the window as the August heat creeps into my room.
Softly at first and then louder and louder, a familiar song fills the air.
CO-QUÍ, CO-QUÍ, CO-QUÍ
"Co-quí, co-quí. Oh, how I love thee!" I sing back.
Luna runs in circles, dancing to our melody.

"Benito, they're singing again!" I shout.
"The coquíes still sing!"

The coquíes' song sounds like home,
even though home has forever changed.

Glossary

hola [**oh**-lah]: greeting meaning "hello"
coquí [koh-**kee**]: tree frog native to Puerto Rico
abuela [ah-**bweh**-lah]: grandmother
pueblo [**pweh**-bloh]: a communal village, town
papi [**pah**-pee]: daddy

Hurricane María

The Coquíes Still Sing takes place in Utuado, Puerto Rico, a town located in the central mountainous area of the island known as La Cordillera Central. Puerto Rico is an archipelago in the Caribbean with a population of approximately three million people. On September 20, 2017, Hurricane María made direct landfall on Puerto Rico and was the strongest hurricane to traverse the archipelago in nearly a century.

Coquí, Coquí

As a result of the hurricane, thousands of lives were lost, more than a million houses were destroyed, and the rain forest, El Yunque, was nearly decimated, including the habitats of the native coquí frogs. The coquí's distinctive mating call has a profound cultural significance for Puerto Ricans. It is typically heard at dusk until dawn across Puerto Rico. For several decades, the population of the coquí frog had been decreasing due to drought and habitat loss incurred from commercial and residential development. However, the coquíes' song fell silent immediately after Hurricane María. It was an alarming sign of the ecological consequences of this catastrophic hurricane.[1] Although the coquíes experienced a dramatic population decline, residents began hearing the slow resurgence of the coquí's song months after Hurricane María.

---

1 *New York Times*, "Another Victim of Hurricane María: Puerto Rico's Treasured Rainforest": 2017. nytimes.com/2017/10/11/us/another-victim-of-hurricane-maria-puerto-ricos-treasured-rainforest.html.

Puerto Rico and the United States

Puerto Rico is not an incorporated state of the United States but rather its territory. Therefore, international humanitarian assistance after Hurricane María was limited, creating a situation in which Puerto Rico relied almost entirely on aid provided by the US.[2] After public and internal political pressure, the United States government agreed to briefly waive the Jones Act, a law prohibiting non-US ships from docking at Puerto Rico's ports to import goods.[3] Years after Hurricane María, families across the archipelago have reported that they still lack basic necessities such as electricity, secure housing, and medical services.[4]

2 *New York Times*, "Puerto Rico's Agriculture and Farmers Decimated by Maria": 2017. nytimes.com/2017/09/24/us/puerto-rico-hurricane-maria-agriculture-.html.

3 *Washington Post*, "Trump just lifted the Jones Act for Puerto Rico. Here's what that does.": 2017. washingtonpost.com/news/the-fix/wp/2017/09/27/all-about-the-jones-act-an-obscure-shipping-law-thats-stalling-puerto-ricos-recovery/.

4 NBC News, "FEMA acknowledges Puerto Rico lacks rebuilt homes and a hospital to survive COVID-19": 2020. nbcnews.com/news/latino/fema-acknowledges-puerto-rico-lacks-rebuilt-homes-hospital-survive-covid-n1234810.

Life After Hurricane María

Despite limited financial resources, the people of Puerto Rico rebuilt their neighborhoods and replanted trees and crops. Mutual aid centers were developed to collect and distribute supplies to those in need.[5] The remote town of Utuado was especially hard hit due to its mountainous terrain, outdated infrastructure, and limited access to medical and construction supplies. Local schools were shut down following a governmental push for public school privatization, which forced many students to commute to schools farther away. Consequently, many families made the decision to leave Puerto Rico. According to the US Census Bureau, it is estimated that 130,000 people have relocated to the United States in the aftermath of Hurricane María.[6]

Food Sovereignty

Puerto Ricans on the islands and in the diaspora continue to seek "just recovery" following Hurricane María, a recovery that advocates for food sovereignty, community self-determination, and more.[7] According to current US law, fruits, vegetables, and meat must be imported from the US even though Puerto Rico has arable land. Economists, farmers, politicians, and activists have been informing the public about the detrimental reliance on US imports for the nutritional sustenance of the Puerto Rican people. Today, there is a renewed drive to reclaim and cultivate *la tierra* to establish agricultural independence from the US.[8]

---

5 NACLA, "Mutual Aid and Survival as Resistance in Puerto Rico": 2020. nacla.org/news/2020/08/07 /mutual-aid-and-survival-resistance-puerto-rico.

6 US Census, "More Puerto Ricans Move to Mainland United States, Poverty Declines": 2019. census.gov/library/stories/2019/09/puerto-rico-outmigration-increases-poverty-declines.html.

7 Climate Justice Alliance, "Our Power Puerto Rico: Moving Toward a Just Recovery": 2019. climatejusticealliance.org/our-power-puerto-rico-report/.

8 Civil Eats, "Farmers in Puerto Rico are Growing a Culture of Social Justice and Climate Resilience": 2020. civileats.com/2020/03/11/farmers-in-puerto-rico-are-growing-a-culture-of-social-justice-and-climate -resilience/.

A Call to Action

In the aftermath of Hurricane María and subsequent earthquakes, grassroots organizations have provided critical services and supplies to the public, including meals, groceries, solar lamps, farming, and reconstruction. There are also organizations dedicated to conservation and biodiversity efforts. Several of these groups are listed below:

Comedores Sociales de Puerto Rico: Self-managed food-distribution initiative based in Caguas focused on eradicating hunger through strategies of collective work and socialization of resources. comedoressocialespr.org

La Maraña: Women-led participatory design and planning organization that helps integrate civilians in the design and recuperation of communities across Puerto Rico. lamarana.org

Taller Salud: A feminist organization based in Loíza dedicated to the health and development of girls and women and their communities. tallersalud.com

La Colmena Cimarrona: Vieques-based collective that practices solidarity economy, agroecology, and beekeeping with the intention of flourishing food sovereignty in the archipelago of Puerto Rico. colmenacimarrona.org

El Departamento de la Comida: Decentralized collective based in San Juan that provides tools, seeds, and educational materials to farmers throughout the island. eldepartamentodelacomida.org

Casa Pueblo: Community-based organization in Adjuntas committed to protecting natural, cultural, and human resources in Puerto Rico. casapueblo.org

Protectores de Cuencas: Community-based nonprofit organization helping to restore and protect watersheds and associated ecosystems across Puerto Rico. protectoresdecuencas.org

Proyecto Coquí: A nonprofit organization whose mission is the conservation of biodiversity in Puerto Rico through scientific research, habitat protection, and environmental education. proyectocoqui.com

Author's Note
Puerto Rico, Te Quiero

As a child, my parents sent me to Puerto Rico each summer to stay with my grandmother in the town of Vega Baja. Every moment in Puerto Rico was a sensorial experience, like the song of the coquíes comforting me each night as I acclimated to the grueling July heat. It is the emblematic sound of Puerto Rico.

Abuela Eva standing in front of her house in Vega Baja, April 2018.

Karina and Abuela Eva in Vega Baja, December 2021.

Growing up, I never found my culture depicted in a picture book. Today, I'm a bilingual speech-language pathologist at a public school in Brooklyn, New York, and while building a library for my therapy room, I realized that still few books reflected the cultures and experiences of my students of color. My students savor stories that describe relatable experiences of hardship and courage. While targeting my students' storytelling skills through therapy, their boundless imaginations inspired this dream to write picture books of my own.

Following the aftermath of Hurricane María, I participated in fundraising efforts for grassroots organizations in Puerto Rico and helped collect picture books for schoolchildren in Cataño, Puerto Rico. These experiences compelled me to write *The Coquíes Still Sing*. It is my hope that this story illuminates and energizes people of all ages and that it sparks a deep love for humanity and the environment. Children's books create learning opportunities not just for children but also for the adults who read with them. This is the magic that I relish.

Karina with her mother, Maritza, and Abuela Eva in Vega Baja, summer of 1992.

Illustrator's Note

I grew up on an entirely different island, New York City, where I would hear stories about the small and mighty coquí frogs, my parents whistling their rhythmic tune before bedtime. Whenever we were in Puerto Rico—visiting family on the west side of the island or traveling to El Yunque National Forest—I always felt at home as the hot, humid nights filled with the sounds of coquíes. In my great-aunt's garden, I was amazed by fruit that grew at arm's reach, so ripe it would cry in the heat of the sun. In the town of Isabela, my cousin introduced me to Pozo de Jacinto, where I saw both how beautiful and terrifying water could be as it crashed up through the cove onto razor-sharp rocks. I had to question why, as a family, we had come to live in a concrete city, and I learned why, even in such a magical place, life could be challenging. As I got older, I became eager to share Puerto Rico's enchantments with friends and loved ones.

Krystal, four years old, sitting on her great-grandmother Angela's lap. (From left to right) Krystal's sister, Lyneve; her mother, Evelyn; and great-aunt, Estrella, in Arecibo, summer of 1995.

In May 2018, I traveled to Puerto Rico with a group of close friends. It was my first trip to the island post–Hurricane María. I witnessed the tremendous effect the category-four hurricane had, resulting in muddy brown rivers, stripped flamboyant trees, shuttered businesses along the shores, and homes that stood exposed to the elements almost a year later. The color of the land was visibly faded, yet the vibrance of Puerto Rico's spirit shone through. With the strikes of machetes, street vendors continued to crack open fresh coconuts, selling sweet tastes of perseverance. A home-cooked meal prepared in Quebradillas by my friend's mother was filled with love and tasted as delicious as anything I've ever experienced.

This story of resilience—the brilliant strength of a people and their land—is what I wanted to capture in *The Coquíes Still Sing*. Karina's story inspired me to look back at photos from my previous travels. I collected personal images from Karina and researched articles and videos from the time of the hurricane to piece together references for my illustrations, hoping to create images that would resonate with the experiences of the many families affected by Hurricane María and its aftermath. My heart lies close to Puerto Rico, and as an artist, I wanted to show that.

Krystal, two years old, with her great-aunt, Estrella, in Aguada, summer of 1993.